HOW TO LIVE FOREVER

COLIN THOMPSON

Alfred A. Knopf · New York

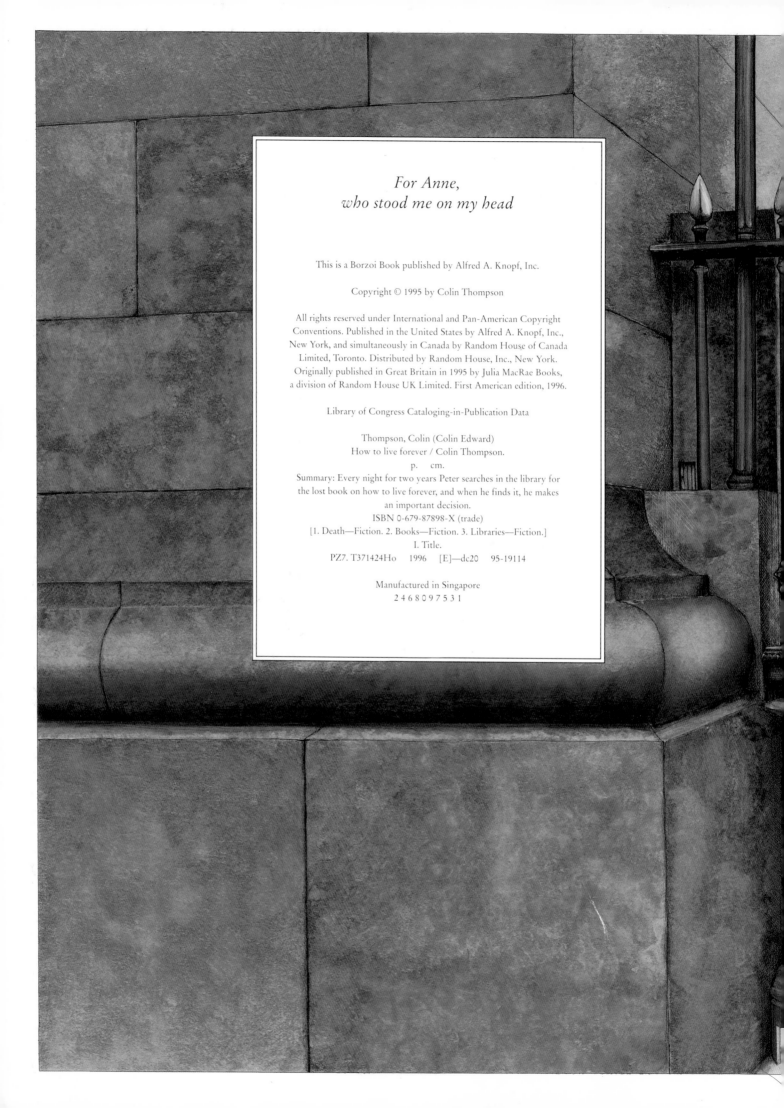

For Anne,
who stood me on my head

This is a Borzoi Book published by Alfred A. Knopf, Inc.

Copyright © 1995 by Colin Thompson

All rights reserved under International and Pan-American Copyright
Conventions. Published in the United States by Alfred A. Knopf, Inc.,
New York, and simultaneously in Canada by Random House of Canada
Limited, Toronto. Distributed by Random House, Inc., New York.
Originally published in Great Britain in 1995 by Julia MacRae Books,
a division of Random House UK Limited. First American edition, 1996.

Library of Congress Cataloging-in-Publication Data

Thompson, Colin (Colin Edward)
How to live forever / Colin Thompson.
p.   cm.
Summary: Every night for two years Peter searches in the library for
the lost book on how to live forever, and when he finds it, he makes
an important decision.
ISBN 0-679-87898-X (trade)
[1. Death—Fiction. 2. Books—Fiction. 3. Libraries—Fiction.]
I. Title.
PZ7. T371424Ho   1996   [E]—dc20   95-19114

Manufactured in Singapore
2 4 6 8 0 9 7 5 3 1

In a quiet street of tall trees there is a library with a thousand rooms. On the shelves are copies of every book that has ever been written.

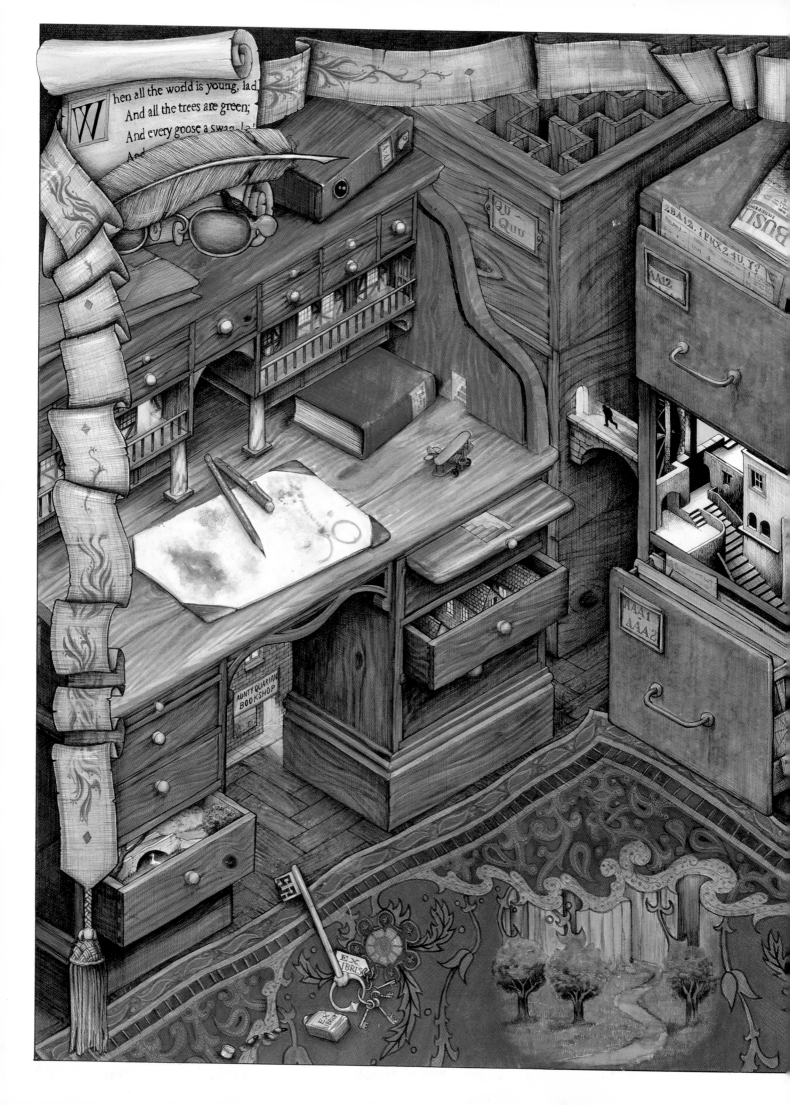

When all the world is young, lad,
And all the trees are green;
And every goose a swan, lad,
And

But one book is missing. Two hundred years ago someone hid its record card under the bottom drawer of a filing cabinet, and the book quietly vanished.

The book is called *How to Live Forever*.

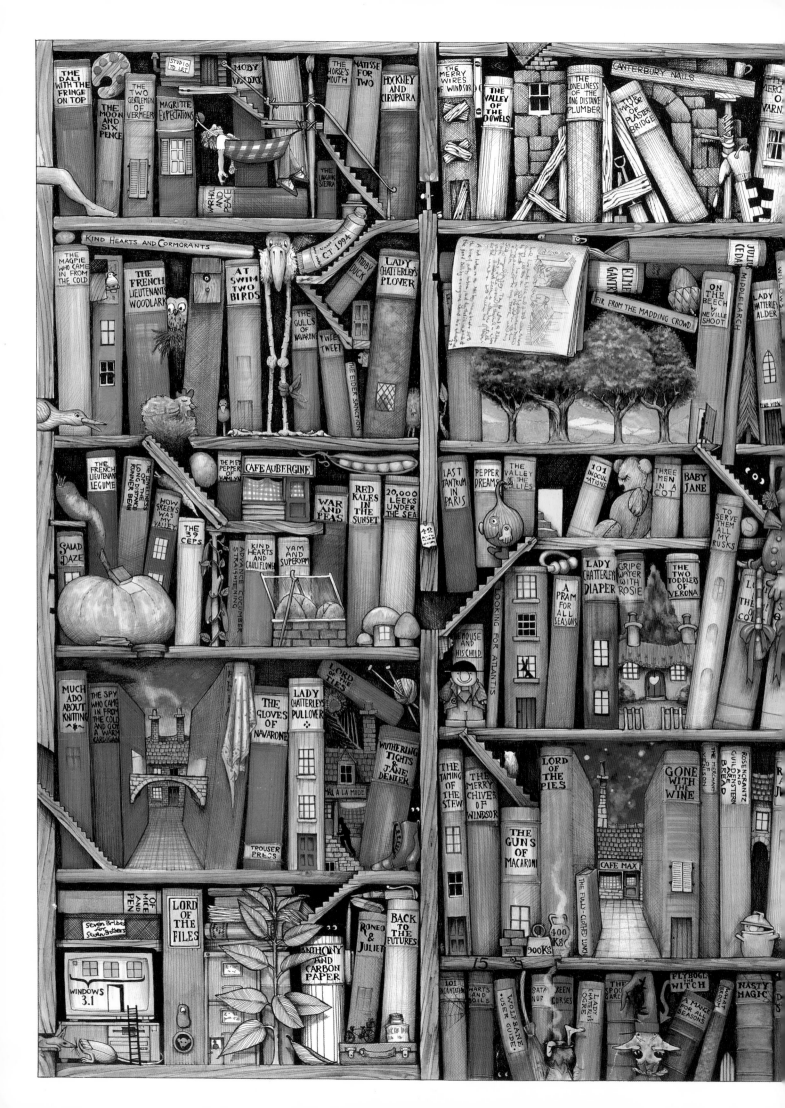

When the library is closed and the night watchman has fallen asleep in his big armchair, the shelves come to life. Doors and windows appear on the backs of the books, lights come on, and the sound of voices drifts out between the pages. Full-grown trees spring up and chimneys begin to smoke. Staircases and ladders join the shelves into great cities, and in the distance small dogs bark.

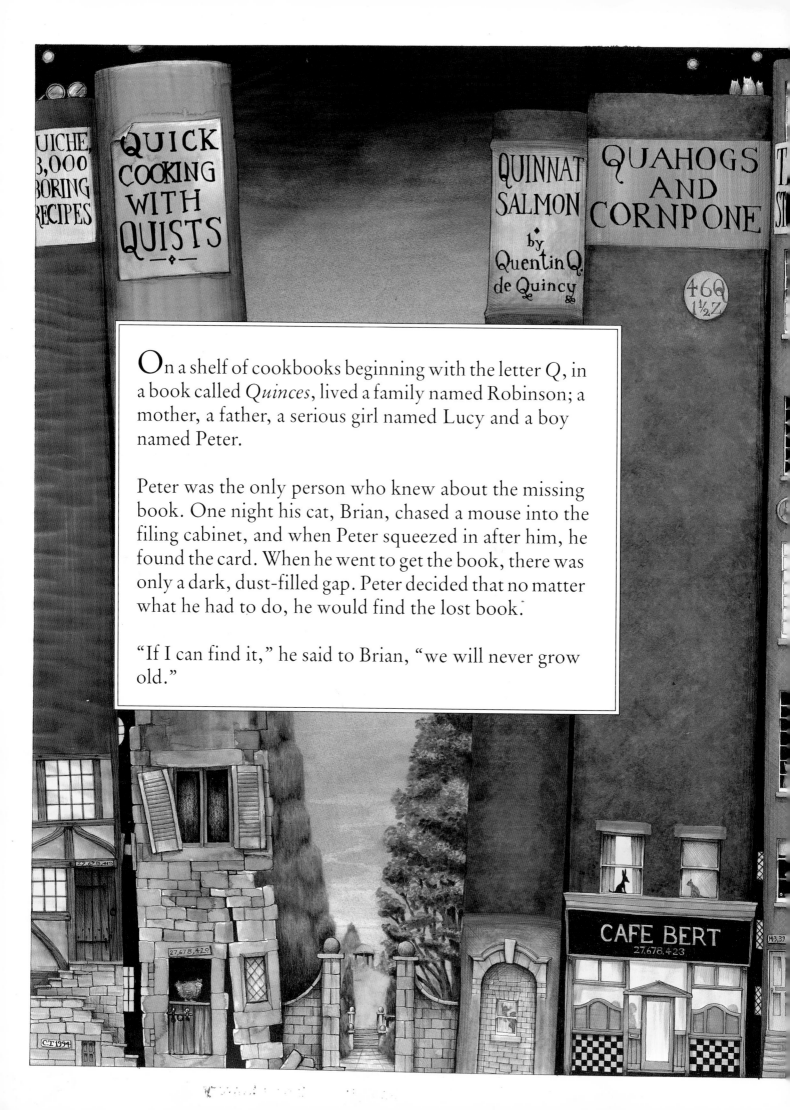

On a shelf of cookbooks beginning with the letter Q, in a book called *Quinces*, lived a family named Robinson; a mother, a father, a serious girl named Lucy and a boy named Peter.

Peter was the only person who knew about the missing book. One night his cat, Brian, chased a mouse into the filing cabinet, and when Peter squeezed in after him, he found the card. When he went to get the book, there was only a dark, dust-filled gap. Peter decided that no matter what he had to do, he would find the lost book.

"If I can find it," he said to Brian, "we will never grow old."

Every night for the next two years Peter and Brian searched for the book.

On the shelves near the empty space there were books about age-old medicines and health books full of exercises and salads. Peter walked past rows of books with people in leotards leaping about, eating celery, and having their thighs photographed. But it was always the same. When he looked closely, they all had wrinkles around their eyes. They were getting older. *They* didn't know about the book.

"Where's that boy off to every night?" said his mother.

"As long as he's not getting into any trouble, it's all right," said his father.

Peter traveled from room to room, through secret cellars of forbidden books to well-worn shelves of cowboy stories, through silent books of Braille to the street guides of lost cities.

And then, on a dark shelf below the ceiling in a long-forgotten attic, Peter found four old men standing ankle-deep in dust, each balanced on one leg in front of a row of ancient Chinese books. The old men had white hair and deeply lined faces. *They* surely didn't know about the book.

Peter watched them. If it hadn't been for their gentle breathing, the old men could have been statues.

"Welcome," said the first old man. He put his foot down very slowly, so as not to disturb the dust, and bowed.

"You are just in time for tea," said the second. He too put his foot on the ground and bowed. The third man did the same. The fourth man didn't move, and when Peter looked closer, he saw that he was asleep.

"We don't get many visitors," said the first old man.

"You're the first," said the second.

Peter followed the old men into a large faded book. It was filled with the scent of spices and ancient memories. Beautiful carpets covered the floors, and red-lacquered shelves crammed with a thousand treasures filled the walls.

"You've come for this, haven't you?" said the third man, holding out a small book.

Peter took it and read the faded words:

How to Live Forever, or *Immortality for Beginners*.

Peter couldn't understand it. If these four old men had the book, why were they so old? He thought for a moment.

"It doesn't work, does it?" he said.

"Oh, yes, it works," said one of the old men.

"Well, why . . ." began Peter.

"Why are we so old?"

"Yes."

"Follow me," said the old man, "and I will show you."

He led Peter through a door into a Chinese garden. It was the most beautiful place the boy had ever seen. Delicate trees shivered in a soft breeze. Their blossoms fell into pools of clear water filled with silent fish. Chinese quail picked across the earth, and bright butterflies flew around his head. Peter just wanted to stand and stare, but the old man was walking off down the path.

"Where are we going?" said Peter, running after him.

"To see the Ancient Child," said the old man.

Peter followed the old man through the trees into a clearing. There, in a large chair, sat the Ancient Child. He was both young and old, ten and timeless at the same time. His skin was as smooth as a child's, but it was dull and tired. His eyes were a child's eyes, but they were weary and far away.

"This young one has come for the book," said the old man.

"You mustn't read it," said the Ancient Child. "It will drive you mad."

"I am the only person," he went on, "who has read it and not lost his mind. I was younger than you when I found it, and I couldn't read it fast enough. Then, while my friends grew up, I stayed like this. They grew out of toys and fell in love. They married and had children, and all I could do was sit and watch. Now I am frozen in time. I keep saying that I had everything, but all I had was endless tomorrows. To live forever is to not live at all. That's why I hid the book."

"Why didn't you just burn it?" asked Peter.

"The book is immortal, too," said the Ancient Child.

Peter walked through the garden feeling quite desolate. When he reached the pool, he sat down on the warm earth. All afternoon he watched the goldfish. They too were growing old, but their children were swimming in their shadows.

"I won't read it," he said, and went back to the Ancient Child.

EX JULIAE LIBRIS
MCMXCIV

"You are wiser than I was," said the Ancient Child,
and led him back to the world.